STAR WARS

THE FORCE AWAKENS
NEW ADVENTURES

Written by David Fentiman

Penguin
Random
House

Written and Edited by David Fentiman
Project Art Editor Owen Bennett
Creative Technical Support Tom Morse
Senior Pre-Production Producer Jennifer Murray
Senior Producer Alex Bell
Managing Editor Sadie Smith
Managing Art Editor Ron Stobbart
Art Director Lisa Lanzarini
Publisher Julie Ferris
Publishing Director Simon Beecroft

For Cameron + Company
Designers Dagmar Trojanek, Amy Wheless and Jillian Lungaro
Creative Director Iain Morris

For Lucasfilm
Executive Editor Jonathan W. Rinzler
Image Archives Stacey Leong
Art Director Troy Alders
Story Group Leland Chee, Pablo Hidalgo and Rayne Roberts

First published in Great Britain in 2015 by
Dorling Kindersley Limited
80 Strand, London, WC2R 0RL
A Penguin Random House Company

10 9 8 7 6 5 4 3 2
002–195846–December/2015

Page design copyright © 2015 Dorling Kindersley Limited

A CIP catalogue record for this book is available from the British Library.

ISBN 978-0-24120-115-2

Printed and bound in China

A WORLD OF IDEAS:
SEE ALL THERE IS TO KNOW

www.dk.com
www.starwars.com

Contents

A NEW BATTLE

The galaxy is in danger!
The evil First Order wants to take over.
Only the Resistance can stop it.

THE RESISTANCE

The brave Resistance fights against the First Order.
General Leia is the leader of the Resistance. She has
many pilots and soldiers to help her. The Resistance
has a secret base on a planet named D'Qar.

THE FIRST ORDER

The First Order is all that remains of the Empire. The evil Empire once ruled the galaxy. It was destroyed many years ago by Leia and her brother, Luke. Now the First Order wants revenge!

Kylo Ren

Kylo Ren is the First Order's greatest warrior. He is very powerful, and very evil. Kylo uses a weapon known as a lightsaber. He also uses the Force. This is a strange energy that gives him special powers!

General Leia

General Leia is also a princess. Many years ago, she fought against the Empire with her brother, Luke. He was a noble warrior known as a Jedi. Luke disappeared a long time ago, and now Leia is trying to find him.

9

C-3PO and R2-D2

R2-D2 and C-3PO are old friends of Leia's. They are both droids. C-3PO serves Leia in the Resistance, but R2-D2 has been shut down for a long time. Ever since his master Luke Skywalker went away, R2 has not spoken to anyone.

Poe Dameron

Poe is General Leia's best pilot.
His ship is called an X-wing.
Poe flies his X-wing with great
skill. Leia sends Poe on a secret
mission to help find her brother,
Luke. Poe is very brave and
would do anything for Leia.

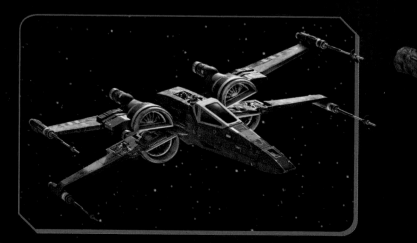

POE'S MISSION

MISSION GOAL 1
Fly to desert planet named Jakku

MISSION GOAL 2
Meet the explorer Lor San Tekka

MISSION GOAL 3
Get secret artefact from Lor and bring it back to Leia

MISSION PLANET Jakku

POSSIBLE DANGERS

- First Order might attack at any time
- Jakku has savage wildlife and dangerous deserts

Finn

Finn was once a stormtrooper.
Stormtroopers are the First
Order's soldiers. His real name
is FN-2187, but his friends call
him Finn. Finn sees how evil
the First Order is, and he decides
to run away.

Rey

Rey comes from the planet Jakku. She works in a junkyard, and never expects to join the Resistance. Rey is an expert at fixing machines. She has built a speeder out of spare parts. Rey slowly realises that she can use the Force.

BB-8

BB-8 is a type of robot called an astromech droid. He helps Poe pilot his X-wing. BB-8 is an unusual droid. His whole body rolls when he moves, but his head stays still! BB-8 is very loyal to Poe.

23

Captain Phasma

Captain Phasma leads the First Order's stormtroopers. She wears special silver armour and is very frightening. The only thing she cares about is destroying the First Order's enemies.

General Hux

General Hux is in charge of the First Order's army and fleet of starships. Hux has built a huge weapon named the Starkiller. He wants to use it to defeat the Resistance.

27

THE STARKILLER

The Starkiller is a giant weapon. It takes up a whole planet! It can smash an entire star system with a single blast. The Starkiller is guarded by thousands of stormtroopers.

- ► Able to destroy
  an entire star system
- ► Shields are very strong
- ► Has very powerful
  defences

- ► Cannot move
- ► Cannot be hidden
- ► If damaged, may
  destroy itself
- ► Takes time to charge up

The Resistance Base

The Resistance base is hidden
on a planet named D'Qar.
The base is where the Resistance
keeps its starships.

The Resistance base also has a command centre. It is buried deep underground. This is where General Leia and her officers plan their battles.

Admiral Statura

Admiral Statura is General
Leia's second-in-command at
the Resistance base. He helps
Leia plan missions against the
First Order. Admiral Statura
is very clever. He knows a lot
about weapons and vehicles.

33

Han Solo and Chewbacca

Han was once a smuggler, but he helped Leia defeat the Empire. He and his co-pilot Chewbacca have been together for a very long time. Their ship is called the *Millennium Falcon*. Han cares for Leia, and he agrees to join the Resistance.

Admiral Ackbar

Admiral Ackbar is one of Leia's officers. He is a Mon Calamari.

He fought beside Leia in the war against the Empire, 30 years ago. They have been through many dangerous battles together. Leia trusts Ackbar with her life.

RESISTANCE PILOTS

PILOT PROFILE
Poe Dameron

RANK: **Commander**

HOMEWORLD: **Yavin 4**

SKILL: **Improvising**

PILOT PROFILE
Snap Wexley

RANK: **Captain**

HOMEWORLD: **Akiva**

SKILL: **Scouting missions**

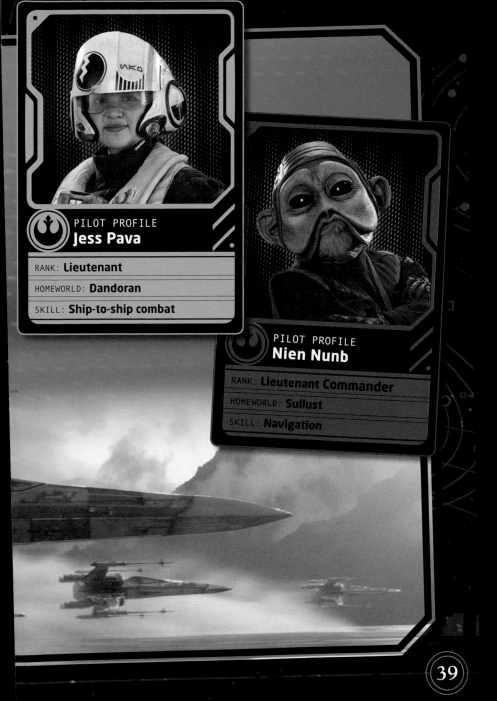

PILOT PROFILE
Jess Pava

RANK: **Lieutenant**

HOMEWORLD: **Dandoran**

SKILL: **Ship-to-ship combat**

PILOT PROFILE
Nien Nunb

RANK: **Lieutenant Commander**

HOMEWORLD: **Sullust**

SKILL: **Navigation**

X-WINGS

Astromech droid

Laser cannon

Cockpit

Nose cone

Engine

Wing

The Resistance flies X-wing starfighters.
X-wings are fast and well armed.
The X-wing pilots must try to
destroy the Starkiller!

Quiz

1. Who is the First Order's greatest warrior?

2. Who leads the Resistance?

3. What is the First Order's giant weapon called?

4. What type of droid is BB-8?

5. What kind of starfighters does
   the Resistance use?

Answers on page 45

Glossary

Droid A robot

The Empire An evil group that once ruled the galaxy

The First Order A powerful army created from the remains of the Empire

The Force A strange and powerful energy that has a light side and a dark side

General Someone who leads soldiers in battle

Jedi Someone who uses the light side of the Force to do good

The Resistance A group that defends the galaxy from the First Order

Smuggler Someone who transports illegal goods

Index

Answers to the quiz on pages 42 and 43:
1. Kylo Ren 2. General Leia 3. The Starkiller
4. An astromech droid 5. X-wings

Guide for Parents

DK Reads is a three-level reading series for children, developing the habit of reading widely for both pleasure and information. These books have exciting running text interspersed with a range of reading genres to suit your child's reading ability, as required by the school curriculum. Each book is designed to develop your child's reading skills, fluency, grammar awareness and comprehension in order to build confidence and engagement when reading.

Ready for a *Beginning to Read* book
YOUR CHILD SHOULD

- be using phonics, including combinations of consonants, such as bl, gl and sm, to read unfamiliar words; and common word endings, such as plurals, ing, ed and ly.

- be using the storyline, illustrations and the grammar of a sentence to check and correct their own reading.

- be pausing briefly at commas, and for longer at full stops; and altering his/her expression to respond to question, exclamation and speech marks.

A Valuable and Shared Reading Experience

For many children, reading requires much effort but adult participation can make this both fun and easier. So here are a few tips on how to use this book with your child.

TIP 1 Check out the contents together before your child begins:

- Read the text about the book on the back cover.

- Read through and discuss the contents page together to heighten your child's interest and expectation.

- Briefly discuss any unfamiliar or difficult words on the contents page.

- Chat about the non-fiction reading features used in the book, such as headings, captions, recipes, lists, or charts.

This introduction helps to put your child in control and makes the reading challenge less daunting.

TIP 2 Support your child as he/she reads the story pages:

- Give the book to your child to read and turn the pages.

- Where necessary, encourage your child to break a word into syllables, sound out each one and then flow the syllables together. Ask him/her to reread the sentence to check the meaning.

- When there's a question mark or an exclamation mark, encourage your child to vary his/her voice as he/she reads the sentence. Demonstrate how to do this if it is helpful.

TIP 3 Praise, share and chat:

- The factual pages tend to be more difficult than the story pages, and are designed to be shared with your child.

- Ask questions about the text and the meaning of the words used. Ask your child to suggest his/her own quiz questions. These help to develop comprehension skills and awareness of the language used.

A FEW ADDITIONAL TIPS

- Try and read together every day. Little and often is best. After 10 minutes, only keep going if your child wants to read on.

- Always encourage your child to try reading difficult words by themselves. Praise any self-corrections; for example, "I like the way you sounded out that word and then changed the way you said it, to make sense".

- Read other books of different types to your child just for enjoyment and information.

Have you read these other great books from DK?

BEGINNING TO READ

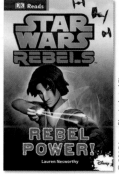

Meet a band of rebels, brave enough to take on the Empire!

Visit a building site and watch the mega machines in action.

Get ready to go on another adventure with the rebels of Lothal!

STARTING TO READ ALONE

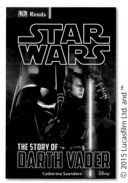

Discover Jupiter with its colourful clouds and awesome moons.

Buckle up and get ready for an action-packed ride!

Uncover the mystery behind Darth Vader's mask.